Emma Thomson's
felicity Wishes

FELICITY WISHES
Text by Emma Thomson
Illustrated by Emma Thomson

With thanks to Emma Layfield and Helen Bailey

British Library Cataloguing in Publication Data
A catalogue record of this book is available from the British Library.
ISBN 0-340-87840-1
Felicity Wishes © 2000 Emma Thomson.
Licensed by White Lion Publishing.
Felicity Wishes: Little book of Christmas © 2003 Emma Thomson.

First HB edition published 2003
10 9 8 7 6 5 4 3 2 1

Published by Hodder Children's Books, a division of Hodder Headline Limited,
338 Euston Road, London, NW1 3BH

Originated by Dot Gradations Ltd, Uk
Printed in China

Emma Thomson's

felicity Wishes

Little book of

Christmas

h
Hodder
Children's
Books

A division of Hodder Headline Limited

Christmas is for sending cards
to your friends.

Use your best fairy handwriting!

Christmas is for decorating your home until it sparkles!

Don't forget the fairy for the top of the tree!

Christmas is for spending time
with friends and family.

Sharing fun and smiles.

Christmas is for treating

your friends.

They really deserve it!

Christmas is for eating all your
favourite things.

And then having more!

Christmas is for making all your

wishes come true.

Wheeeeeeeeee!

Christmas is for hanging up

your stocking.

Don't forget to leave a carrot out for Santa's reindeer!

Christmas is for hoping for

something special.

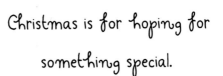

May all your wishes come true.

With this book comes a special
Christmas wish:

Hold the book in your hands and close
your eyes tight.

Count backwards from ten and
when you reach number one, whisper
your wish . . .

. . . but make sure no one can hear.

Keep this book in a safe place and,
maybe, one day, your wish will come true.

Christmas Wishes

felicity

x